Merry
Christmas
Jen

Love,
Laura

December
2001

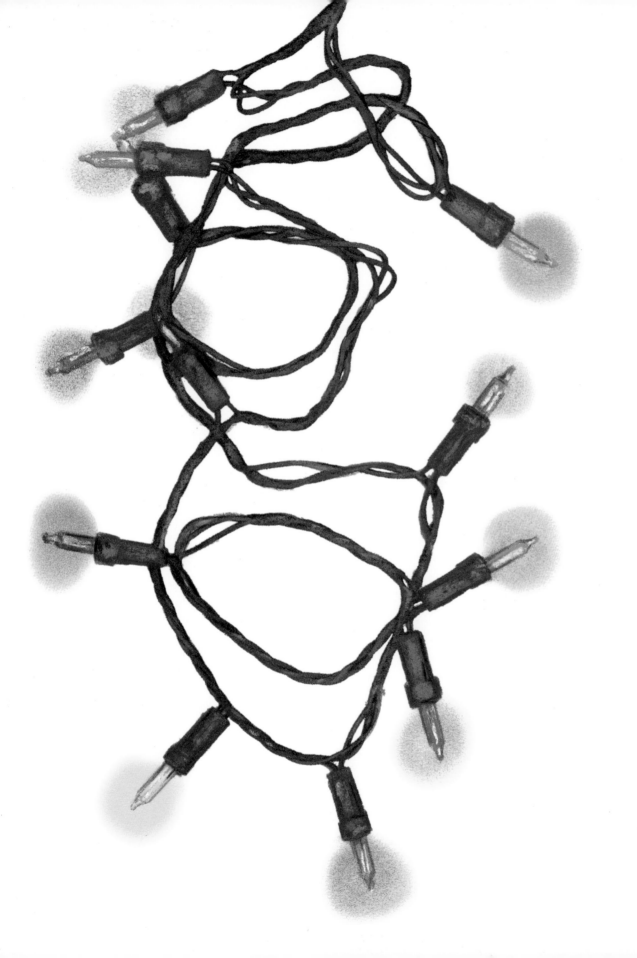

ORNAMENTS

🕯 *Twelve Tales of Christmas* 🕯

ORNAMENTS

❦ *Twelve Tales of Christmas* ❦

Written and illustrated by

KAREN ENGELMANN

SMITHMARK

This edition published in 1998 by SMITHMARK Publishers, a division of
U.S. Media Holdings, Inc., 115 West 18th Street, New York, NY 10011.

SMITHMARK books are available for bulk purchase for sales promotion
and premium use. For details write or call the manager of special sales,
SMITHMARK Publishers, 115 West 18th Street, New York, NY 10011 212-519-1300.

Produced by Karen Engelmann/Luminary Books & Design, Dobbs Ferry, NY

Printed in Hong Kong

10 9 8 7 6 5 4 3 2 1

Library of Congress Cataloging-in-Publication Data
    Engelmann, Karen, 1954-
    Ornaments: twelve tales of Christmas / written and illustrated by
    Karen Engelmann.—1st Smithmark ed.
        p. cm.
    ISBN 0-7651-0869-0 (alk. paper)
    1. Christmas—Fiction. I. Title.
    PS3555.N4103076 1998   98-19564
    813'.54--dc21   CIP

Editorial Director: Elizabeth Viscott Sullivan
Editor: Marisa Bulzone
Production Editor: Tricia Levi

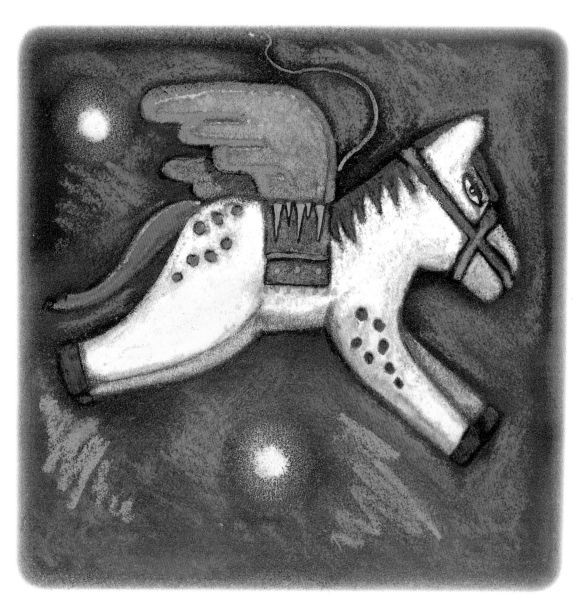

For Margaret

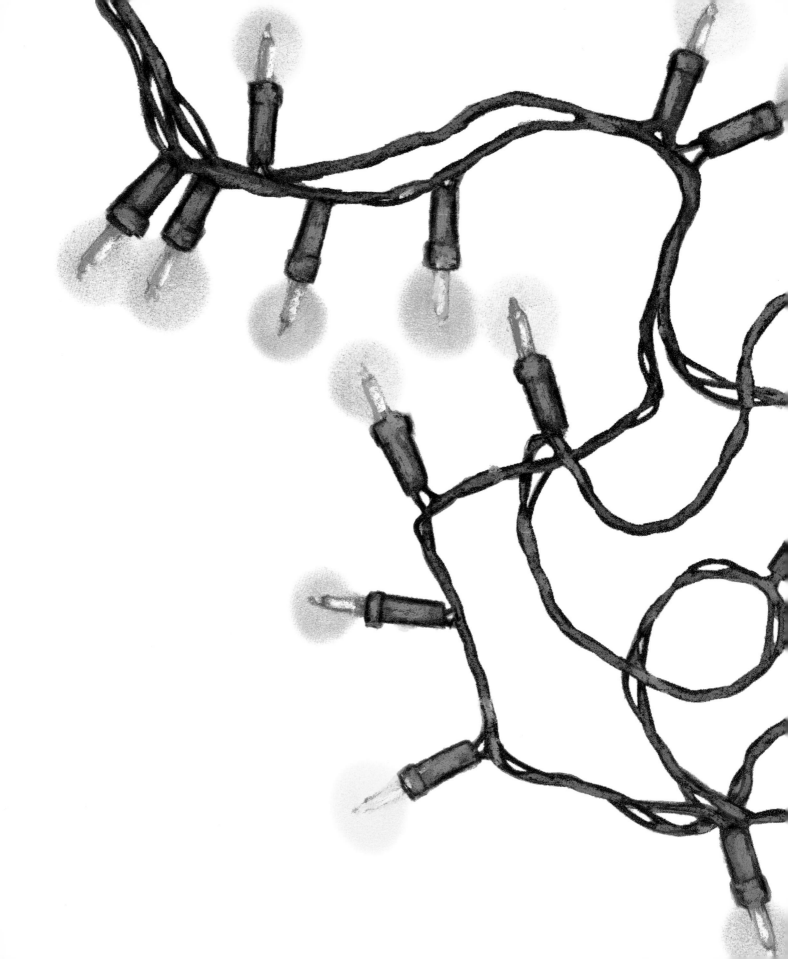

❧ THE TWELVE TALES ❧

THE PERFECT TREE *an introduction*   8

Balls   11

The Angel   17

Tea Time   21

Holiday Found   27

Nice Kitty   33

A Star   39

Accessories   43

The Elf   49

Big Ballerina   55

Flight   59

Wings   65

The Cookie Cycle   69

an introduction

Margaret was squinting at the tree, bent with concentration. "All these huge, empty spaces," she muttered, as she did every year. It was her prelude to a proposed shopping excursion. "We'll have to buy more birds. And those iridescent purple balls—I adore them."

"Everyone has their favorites, but what do you like absolutely best about our Christmas tree?" I said, trying to avoid another trip to Xmas Island, or wherever it was she had in mind.

"I like absolutely all of it," she answered emphatically. It was true: No one more adored the custom of the tree, from beginning to end. And Margaret had been putting them up and taking them down for eighty years, almost a quarter century of that with my family. She had been my husband's college professor, and became his mentor, champion, and good friend. When we first met, Margaret and I had a cordial but wary acquaintanceship, like having an extra mother-in-law.

But over the years we developed an understanding, then a respect, and finally a deep friendship. Eventually she had been transformed to Grandma Margaret and, as the attendant family elder, she directed the yearly ritual of the tree.

The ritual began with the purchase, ten or twelve days before Christmas. If she couldn't visit her Uncle Reginald's four-thousand acre forest and chop down a fine young balsam (for she preferred its spacious branches for hanging ornaments), then the journey to some local church parking lot, transformed for a few cold weeks into a fragrant woods, was undertaken with great seriousness. Freshness was paramount. There was much shaking of frozen branches, and squeezing and smelling of needles. Height was important, too: As tall as the ceiling would allow was the rule, even though she was always outraged at the price. Once the tree was chosen, after what seemed like hours of stamping about in the freezing dark, we would turn to the task of decorating.

The trimming itself was a three-day process, if you allowed a half-day for the two-zillion lights. The rest of the time was for the ornaments. The work was fairly democratic, but we all had favorites we tried to get ahold of first. They were the ornaments that had some strong pull of memory or fantasy, stories we knew deep inside. Certain trimmings were, by unspoken agreement, for Margaret only to hang. Seniority did prevail, and they were handed over with some sense of formality.

It was important to find the perfect place for them. The combinations needed to be just so. We would sometimes find her standing on a chair, moving things that weren't hung quite right. And she insisted on a 360-degree tree: The back had to be as beautiful and jam-packed as the front. There was somehow always room for more.

"Okay," I said to Margaret, "get your coat. Is it Xmas Island or True Value?"

It was—and still is every Christmas—a genuine search for perfection. Not the fashionable look of the current magazines, but a search for the perfect layering of memory. For that, Margaret says, is the point. When you know each and every story of each and every ornament, and they are placed in just such a way that they create a glittering, magical portrait of your life, the decoration is done. You have a perfect tree, full of tales.

Here are a dozen that I look for every year. ❧

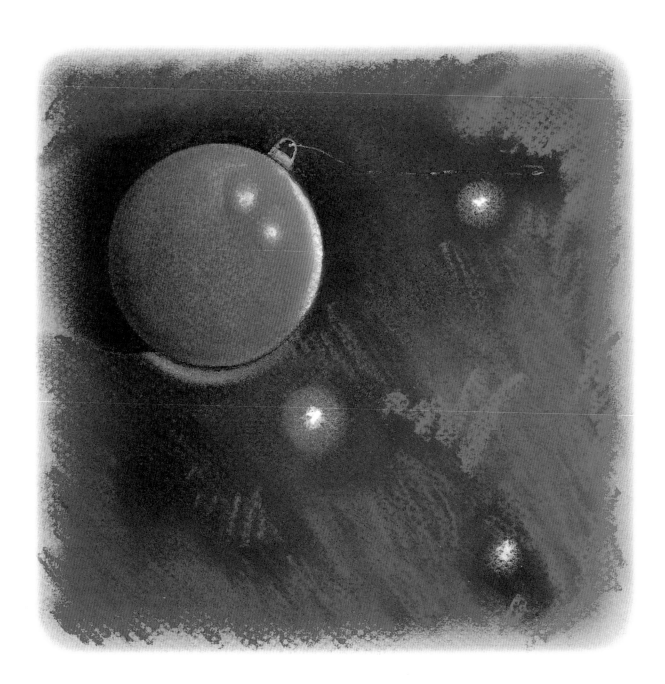

*E*arly November is a lovely time to visit Cape Cod; its muted gray and brown landscape, the sleepy quality of the small towns without the rush of summer bathers, the aura of Pilgrims and witch hunts all combine in an atmosphere of seductive melancholy. It's a wonderful place to spend a fall weekend, to breathe the sea air surrounded by the last taste of autumn before the hysteria of the holidays begin. With that in mind, we planned a weekend visit to our friend Margaret on the Cape. We would take a long drive on the off roads under a sullen gray sky that would blow off to brilliant blue, visit a small museum or two, find a few treasures in some little antique shops, and eat just-caught seafood in harborside restaurants hung with netting and glass floats.

We would wear jeans and boots and sweaters, walk in the woods with the crunch of brown leaves underfoot, and finish the day with homemade apple pie and cheddar cheese, while Margaret told us stories of her family ghosts. There would be no carols, no sprinkly sugar cookies and eggnog, no packages with ribbons, no red velveteen or lacey holiday finery, and no talk of Christmas—not yet.

Saturday was overcast, just as we had hoped. The morning would be perfect for indoor activities, and we could walk in the woods all afternoon once the weather cleared. We headed for a quaint old fishing town just south of the Sagamore bridge. Margaret said it had some splendid architecture that was being restored, a couple of museums, and loads of charm, and there would surely be some cozy restaurant by the water. We took the winding back roads whenever we could to avoid the rush of the Interstate and soon found ourselves opposite The Yankee Captain Antiques, an old saltbox house that had been converted to a shop. As we stepped out of the car it began to sprinkle. "Bosh!" exclaimed Margaret. "A few little Cape Cod drops. It's over by noon!"

There was an antique sleigh out front festooned in red and green ribbons and piled with pine boughs. "Rushing the season a bit, aren't they?" I said to my husband, annoyed that the autumn-splendor mood I envisioned had been violated.

Inside, the proprietress, dressed in a starchy blue shirtwaist and gray cardigan, gave us a perfunctory smile. "Hello. Are you collecting Colonial pieces?" she asked, having already decided we were not. We looked a little too outdoorsy to be serious shoppers. And this shop was serious: nothing later than 1800 and nothing less than $3,000.

We walked respectfully through all the rooms of the shop, silent but for the ticking of a pendulum clock, and always under the watchful eye of the owner. I picked up a small pewter mug priced at about nine grand. "It's all bent up," I said loudly, trying to be funny and sounding

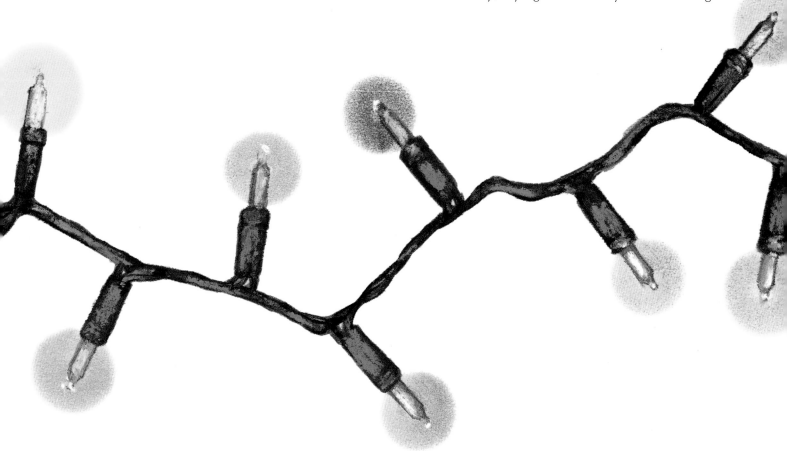

like a complete idiot. The clock chimed. My husband nodded toward the door. "We're visiting the museum," he explained to the shopkeeper, as if asking to be excused.

The museum opened at 11:00, and we had time for a nice stroll down the Main Street. But the drizzle hadn't let up yet, so we hurried to the square and into the Towne Hall Museum. We wandered through the maze of displays and reconstructed rooms, and viewed hundreds of portraits that, after two hours, all looked like George and Martha Washington. At the conclusion of that morning's slide presentation on Windsor chairs, we found ourselves back at the entrance, slightly dazed and hungry. It was time to find some lunch.

The drizzle had become a full-fledged rain. We ran to the car and began a slow circle through town to find the right restaurant—something warm and inviting, with fresh lobster, a harbor view, and a fireplace. We drove around and around and around, growing crabbier and hungrier until we spotted a curbside sandwich

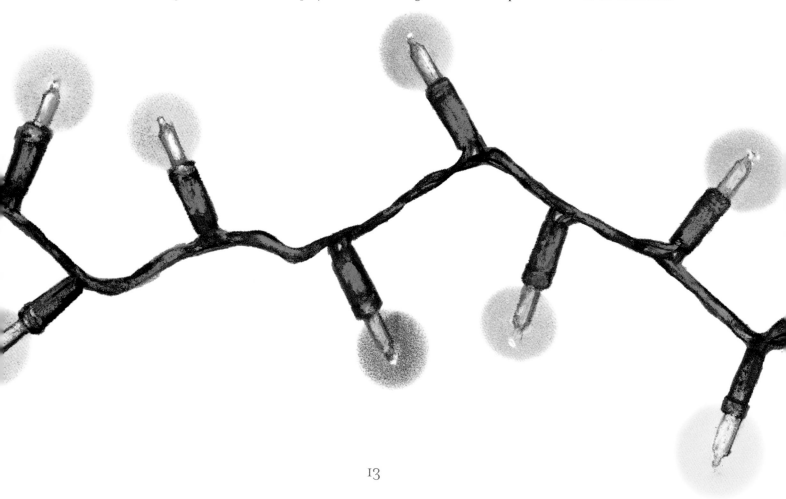

board with a cardboard and Magic Marker sign: PIZZA & DONUTS. Sitting in an orange vinyl booth, the surrounding walls hung with plastic pine boughs, we waited for the rain to let up and polished off a large Pepperoni Special. We asked our waitress if there wasn't another museum in town. "Yeah, Pilgrim House, but it's only open through October," she said. "The Factory Outlets are popular now. Holidays are almost here, ya know." "Halloween was last week," I protested.

We got a bag of donuts to go and headed for New Bedford. "I think there's a Whaling Museum," Margaret said. "But I'm not absolutely sure where it is." The Interstate was lined with billboards that beckoned elsewhere: DESIGNER FASHIONS! THOUSANDS OF SHOPPES! ALL CREDIT CARDS WELCOME! It was pouring now, and traffic was heavy. "It's absurd—people shopping for the holidays. They start so early, it's a scandal," I scolded, peering through the water streaming down the windshield. "Oh heck, we may as well stop until the rain lets up. We can ask about the museum."

The parking lot was jammed, and inside hoards of shoppers roamed under strands of twinkling lights hung among the fluorescent fixtures while lite versions of Christmas carols played subliminally in the background. We wandered aimlessly for a time, then started to walk a bit faster, keeping pace with the carols and the

crowd. All thoughts of Pilgrims and witches and whaling boats were fading, as I gradually succumbed to my surroundings. I found myself mentioning aloud that holiday shopping was maybe not such a bad idea. We started to look in earnest, quickening the pace and shopping like it was Christmas Eve. The sweaters meant for the woods were too hot. Stripped down to T-shirts and jeans, the rustle of autumn leaves was replaced by the rustle of shopping bags, and homemade apple pie with a slice of cheddar was not on the snack bar menu. We settled for nachos and diet sodas, and sucked on free candy canes from the information booth while we proudly surveyed our piles of holiday bargains. The Muzac was on its fourth repeat of "Little Drummer Boy." Time to go.

Like hunters with their quarry, we dragged our bags to the car and flung them into the trunk, then slumped into the cold seats and rummaged for leftover donuts, humming softly to ourselves. Pa-rum-pa-pum-pum.

"Well, since everyone is in the spirit, there *is* a pre-season blow-out at Osco Drugs, just off Highway 6 at the mall," Margaret said as she flicked on the windsheild wipers. "It's right on the way home, and we desperately need more colored balls for the Christmas tree."

We cruised by McDonald's drive-up window for coffee to wash down the donuts, and sped along the Interstate, zipping past the exit for the Whaling Museum. Once at the mall, we were thrilled to get a doorside parking spot and raced inside. It was hot and steamy from the rain and the crush of bodies. We were faced with a confusion of choices, but after a moment we turned as one toward the siren song of electronic carols beckoning us to Osco Drugs.

We headed for the holiday aisle. Two dozen five-foot tall, light-up Santas towered over us on the top shelf, as we were serenaded by the sound of a hundred computerized bells, playing twelve different carols, all at different times. Around us was a bower of synthetic pines, heavy with the scent of balsam deoderizer. One lonely, life-size plastic baby Jesus smiled up at us from a vacuum-formed manger, his strangely adolescent face lit from within by a 60-watt bulb. Above his head was the object of our search: boxes and boxes of shiny red, green, and blue Christmas balls. Twelve for $2.50, a price we all agreed was miraculous. I bought ten boxes.

Hosanna in the highest. The holiday season had begun. 🌿

THE ANGEL

There was a tradition of drawing names for Christmas gifts in our family. With eight children, it was too many presents for one kid to buy, especially if you were, say, a baby of two. Even the older ones, with their paper routes and babysitting money, had a tough time getting something for everyone. They usually tried, though, since it gave them instant status as demi-gods with the rest of us, and masses of brownie points with our parents. But officially, we held a drawing at Thanksgiving. Eight slips of paper were placed into a wicker bread basket, the name you chose was to be kept top secret.

You hoped to be picked by one of the two oldest—they had more cash. Or the baby—Mom always bought the presents from the baby, so you could be pretty sure of a decent gift. The middle kids were all touch and go, myself included. I would spend hours in Woolworth's inspecting all the possibilities—three hankies for $1.25, .5 ounce Evening in Paris toilet water, Play-Doh, slithery nylon socks, cut-glass bud vases at 69¢—hoping to find gifts that seemed nifty and fit my budget. Every penny had to be stretched: There were parents and grandparents to buy for, the teacher at school, Great-Aunt Gen, and, of course, The Name.

If you drew Brian, the baby, or one of the little ones—Huck or Jeff— you were safe in spending a minimum amount. Kids aged 0 and 6 would be happy just opening a package, and instantly forget what the gift was and who gave it to them.

The middle kids—Matt, Gary and I—might throw the present under the tree in disgust, but there was a good chance of success with Silly Putty or a Slinky.

The older two were a challenge. They had sophisticated wish lists, with things like albums and surfer shirts. And the gift needed to please, or there might be a price to pay, usually in the form of exclusion from cooler, big-kid activities that took place around the holiday break.

The year that I was eight, I felt particularly lucky. There was a little extra money from some snow shoveling I had done, so I'd bought extravagant gifts. And rumor had it my oldest brother, Rick, had drawn my name. It would be a flush Christmas all around. The presents were placed under the tree for preliminary squeezing on the afternoon of Christmas Eve, to be opened that night. As the clock ticked toward dinner time, I felt a knot tighten in my stomach. There was only one gift for me, from my older sister Ailleen—she, the teenage goddess of generosity, had bought something for everyone. There should be one more! I knew that there were often last-minute wrappings and small crises with the tape supply, so there was still time.

"Cartoons are on!" I heard someone yell from the basement. The knot in my stomach caught fire. I vividly recalled last week's battle with Rick. He had taken control of the TV three afternoons in a row, interrupting *Captain Ernie's Cartoon Showboat* like some pirate swooping in on three innocent younger siblings. So, I told. Tattle-tale, stool pigeon, rat: He called me that and worse—much worse. I felt a premonition of disaster.

It was getting dark outside now, and the lights from the tree reflected back into the room from the picture window, along with the image of my sad face. I placed my packages under the tree and made one last check of the now-huge pile of presents. There was still only one box waiting there for me.

I went up to my bed and lay down, waiting for dinner, hoping that in my absence the missing gift would materialize. It was dark and still, the room lit only with the orange plastic Christmas candles in the window. The house was waiting for the festivities to begin. Then came the call to dinner.

We had the evening meal, a rush to clean up, and the gathering around the tree. With a stack of Firestone Christmas records on the stereo, my parents settled into their places on the couch and the pandemonium began. Ailleen, the oldest, calling out names, passing out the gifts. Paper flying, ripping, crying, giggling, pulling. Excited laughter. Happiness. I sat with the box from my sister and waited as the pile got smaller and smaller. Eventually the little kids drifted off to play with their toys. My parents opened their boxes of hankies and socks and Evening in Paris, and beamed. I thanked my sister for the lovely long scarf she had knitted in my favorite blue colors, and looked sheepishly under the tree.

"What are you looking for, honey?" my mother asked. I felt small and petty, unable to let go of that missing gift.

"Well, I was wondering who had my name," I said.

"Didn't you get your gift? That's strange. Let me check the list." And like some very efficient Mrs. Claus, she went downstairs to her desk and rummaged around in the files. I tagged along, anxious to discover what I had suspected all along. "Rick," she said, studying her shorthand notes. "Richard Charles!" she yelled as she marched back upstairs to the living room. The only answering sound was Perry Como—"Do you hear what I hear...". Then Rick popped his head around the corner.

"Didn't you have Karen's name?" my mother asked. "Oh, yeah," he answered with studied nonchalance, and disappeared upstairs. A few minutes later he returned, and handed over a small white unwrapped box. "Merry Christmas," he said, not even looking at me. I was staring at the tree, both of us embarrassed at this travesty of the season. We were old enough to know better. He turned and went to the basement to play with the other kids. I stood for the longest time just holding the box. "Well, honey, open it," said my mother. "I'm sure he just forgot."

I opened the box, and inside was a gold pin, an angel with bright blue stones for eyes and a goofy smile, holding a trumpet. As a confirmed tomboy, it couldn't have been further off the mark. I put it back in the box, placed the box under the tree, and went to join the other kids.

All the other gifts from those Christmases have blurred together in my memory, what I gave and what I got. The feelings of excitement, anticipation, delight, and even dread still come back to me, but all the presents are gone: the Barbie clothes, books, stuffed animals, and games. The angel pin, though—I have it still. The trumpet has broken off, but the angel looks as happy as ever, and I see now, when I hang it on the tree at Christmas, that the blue eyes were surely meant to match mine. ❧

TEA TIME

ook what I found way back under the tree! It's for your niece," I said to my husband, holding up a small box wrapped with recycled paper—meaning last year's gift wrap, complete with tears and tape, and half of a ripped-off label with the words To FREDERICK, SEASONS GREE crossed out. It was the day after Christmas and all of the presents had long since been opened. There was no sound when I shook the little box, but the silver bow with white plastic wedding bells clinked as it fell off. "Oh, that has to be from Aunt Rosemary. She recycles everything," he replied. "Sometimes you even get last year's gift—I mean the one she gave you. I don't know how she does it: one day it's deep in your darkest closet, then Christmas comes and it's wrapped and under the tree again. Magic!"

"It's so thoughtful of her to send anything at all. She shouldn't keep doing this."

"I agree completely, especially after getting closet deodorizers two years in a row. What does the label say?" He took the package and read aloud. "To SUZANNA, A CUP OF CHRISTMAS CHEER,

LOVE, AUNT ROSEMARY. It's probably one of those little bottles of Absolut Vodka from the airplane. You know how she hoards that stuff," he laughed.

"Honey, she doesn't hoard it, she drinks it," I noted. "But if she gives Suzanna a bottle of vodka we will really have to tell her she can't keep doing this. Nicely, of course."

We all loved Aunt Rosemary. She lived in the small town in Illinois where she had moved decades ago with her husband Bob. She had a head full of stories and a house full of junk; she saved everything, including her 1958 hairdo, which she maintained with military precision.

"No indeed, I will not!" she would say when we would urge her to make a change. "This was my finest moment! Besides, it all comes around again." I laughed at her for a while, but eventually had to admit she was right. Rosemary was not only ahead of her time, she was ready when it caught up to her again. Suzanna, who was sixteen and her goddaughter, wanted all her old clothes, but Rosemary still wore some of them on occasion. She had managed to keep her figure, too.

"Suzanna, come here. You have a package," I yelled up the stairs. Suzanna was staying with us for a few days during Christmas break. It was a little dull for her, but at least it was a change of authority figures. She came galloping down the stairs at the mention of the word package.

"Who's it from?" she asked breathlessly. "Ooohhhh, it's Great Aunt Rosemary. She's my godmother you know. Maybe she sent me one of her old diamond circle broaches, or that big turquoise cocktail ring. She's too old to drink cocktails anymore anyway!" My husband and I exchanged looks. Suzanna shook the box. "Too quiet. Maybe that huge silk scarf with scenes from Venice. I would love that!" She ripped into the box, pulled out a ball of old newspapers, and carefully peeled them off layer by layer.

"What is it?" we asked.

*S*uzanna turned to us. "What is it?" she repeated, and held up a teacup, or a replica of a teacup, in pink-and-white crochet. "She has gone completely bonkers," said Suzanna with an air of finality. "Gonzo. And I'm supposed to send a thank-you card for this old lady...thing? You keep the teacup. I'm going to watch TV." She dropped the cup and threw a wad of newspaper at the wall as she headed for the stairs.

"Come on, be a sport. You know she adores you. We'll phone her tomorrow—together," I called after her.

She was already gone. "That child has gone sour on us," I told my husband as I picked it up, pulled a ball of yellowed tissue paper from inside the cup and tossed the paper in the pile of torn wrapping. "Still, it is a weird gift for Suzanna. Are you supposed to fill it with those hard candies no one ever eats, or stick in a little potted African violet? What could she have been thinking?" I picked up the pile of papers. "Let's stoke up the fire."

"No, it's late," he yawned. "And Aunt Rosemary would rather you re-use that wrapping paper, but recycling is an acceptable alternative."

I hung the teacup on the tree for lack of an African violet, stuffed the papers in the recycling box, and headed for bed.

The next day I urged Suzanna to call Aunt Rosemary. "She'll be hurt if we don't, and besides, she's probably wondering why we didn't call her on Christmas day."

Suzanna refused. "No way. What could I possibly say about a crocheted teacup. Why don't you call for me and tell her I have the flu."

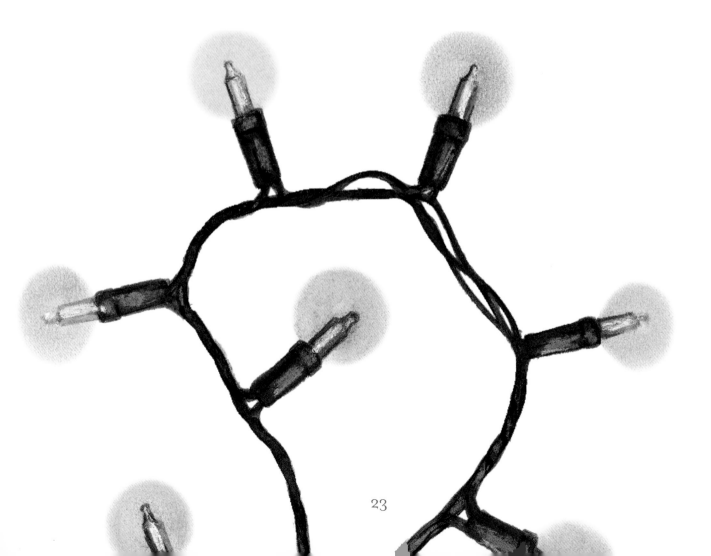

23

"I'm not calling for you. Have some feeling for heaven's sake! She loves you!" I pleaded.

"Sweet, but gonzo." Suzanna went to get her coat, then called from the front hall. "Okay, okay. I'm going to the mall right now, but I'll call her tonight. I promise."

Nobody called poor Aunt Rosemary that night. Or the night after that. When Suzanna left on Friday she wouldn't take the teacup, and she didn't want to call. "I'll write a thank you note when I get home, I promise," she said.

I harrassed my husband. "This is terrible. She's your niece. You have to intervene here!"

"Okay, okay, I'll call Aunt Rosemary. I can say Happy New Year, and tell her that Suzanna loved the teacup so much she was speechless."

"Very lame," I said. "But I don't care. Just do something, please."

He called Aunt Rosemary that evening and had a long, lively chat. They talked about the tea cup and Aunt Rosemary's fondness for a certain Harrod's Tea No. 14. She was reminiscing about London. She re-told her famous old fish story of meeting Lord Whozeewhatsit in 1957 and his wanting to marry her on the spot. He had a special ring made for her at Garrards on Regent Street. But she already loved Uncle Bob, and landed in Illinois. So she said. My husband nodded and uh-huhed his way through forty-five minutes of this, then sat up unnaturally straight. He was getting to the excuses for Suzanna.

"We all loved the teacup," he paused. "Well, she didn't have time to call. Maybe she was embarrassed to say anything because she didn't send you a gift. You know how kids can be." He looked a bit puzzled. "Uh, no. No." He listened intently. "I'm positive nobody saw a teabag. But I'll find out. Yes, I swear it. Yes, cross my heart. Bye-bye, Aunt Rosemary. I'll let you know." He hung up the phone with a strange look on his face. "She said we all missed the Christmas cheer. She said there was a very special teabag inside. Did you see a teabag?"

"Just a wad of yellow tissue paper I dumped in the recycling pile. It's out on the curb now."

He put on his coat and boots, got a flashlight, and was out the door.

"Are you nuts?" I yelled after him. "It's five degrees and pitch dark outside, and you're looking for a teabag?"

"I promised the old darling I would find it. She said it was her dying wish, although of course she's good for another thirty years. She made me swear on my mother's grave."

"But your mother's fine," I called. Mom and Rosemary had never gotten along.

He was out for an hour, and dragged all the boxes back into the garage after an unsuccessful search. "I'll look tomorrow. It's my day off."

He eventually found the wrapping papers, the wedding bow, and the rolled up ball of tissue. Inside there was indeed a teabag, Harrod's No. 14. And tied to the string of the teabag was a magnificent ring. It was an ornate, old-fashioned setting made of silver and very yellow 18-karat gold, and between two small rubies and a smattering of tiny diamond baguettes perched a breathtaking, probably two-carat, rose-cut diamond. Just my size.

We called Aunt Rosemary and told her the whole story. She thought Suzanna was acting a bit immature, and perhaps wasn't ready for such gifts. I was thrilled. We did tell Suzanna, eventually: When she graduated from college some years later. And she insisted we keep the teacup in exchange for the ring. 🌾

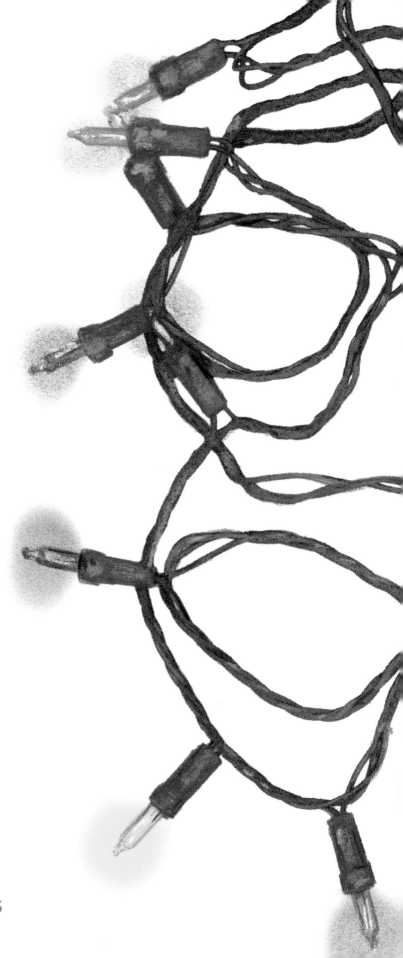

HOLIDAY FOUND

*I*t didn't matter that I was an adult: in my heart, I may as well have been six. At six, I was old enough to have an idea of what the holiday meant and what I liked, and the six-year-old inside of me had the uncomfortable feeling that this year wouldn't be quite right. I pretended to be mature and understanding; I was visibly miserable and confused. It was a little depressing. I wasn't used to the darkness or the incessant rain of Scandinavia, and spending the first semester abroad meant missing Christmas at home. I missed the holiday build up that started in early November: the carols in the grocery store, the millions of lights, a family party or an office party or any excuse to buy eggnog. I even missed the hectic pace, the anxiety over gifts, the indigestion from too many rich holiday treats.

The Christmas season in Sweden was much more subdued and even Santa was conspicuously absent. When you went to the little fake gingerbread house on the square to drop off your wish list, you ended up handing it off to an old bag who called herself The Pepper Cookie Mother.

I lived with my boyfriend in a tiny fourth floor walk-up, facing the interior courtyard of an old apartment building. The courtyard had long ago been turned into a combination parking lot and garbage area for the residents. It was painted a dull grayish-white, which almost matched the color of the never-changing sky

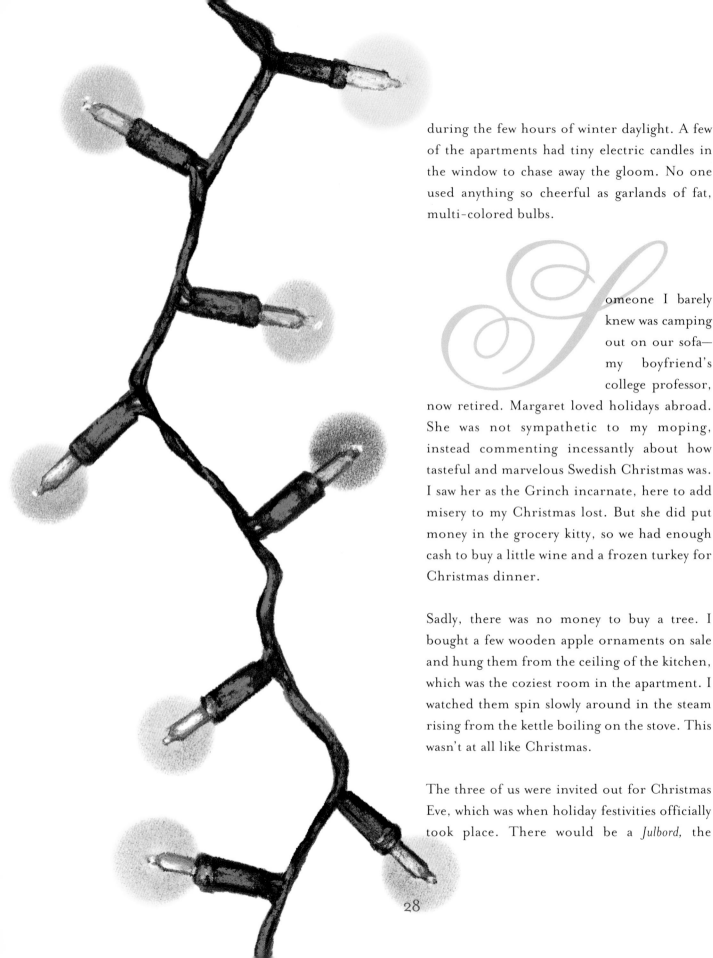

during the few hours of winter daylight. A few of the apartments had tiny electric candles in the window to chase away the gloom. No one used anything so cheerful as garlands of fat, multi-colored bulbs.

Someone I barely knew was camping out on our sofa— my boyfriend's college professor, now retired. Margaret loved holidays abroad. She was not sympathetic to my moping, instead commenting incessantly about how tasteful and marvelous Swedish Christmas was. I saw her as the Grinch incarnate, here to add misery to my Christmas lost. But she did put money in the grocery kitty, so we had enough cash to buy a little wine and a frozen turkey for Christmas dinner.

Sadly, there was no money to buy a tree. I bought a few wooden apple ornaments on sale and hung them from the ceiling of the kitchen, which was the coziest room in the apartment. I watched them spin slowly around in the steam rising from the kettle boiling on the stove. This wasn't at all like Christmas.

The three of us were invited out for Christmas Eve, which was when holiday festivities officially took place. There would be a *Julbord,* the

Christmas smorgasbord, at the beautiful home of a friend's warm-hearted family, most of whom I could not speak with beyond basic pleasantries and asking for a cheese sandwich. My boyfriend knew everyone very well; he had met them during his year as an exchange student in Sweden and felt quite at home. Margaret, who had been studying Swedish in her spare time, chattered on ad nauseum about how delicious everything looked and how much more fun this was than a boring American Christmas dinner. Sitting at the big formal table, faced with lutefish and unidentifiable meat patés, I prayed for the turkey. I longed for canned cranberries. Even Aunt Peggy's green bean casserole. I went to the bathroom for a quick bawl and then composed myself for the rest of the evening. There was always tomorrow.

It was after 11:00 when we returned home. The temperature had dropped, and the solid ceiling of clouds had parted here and there to reveal a trace of stars. More of the windows had their little white candles lit, and it was as still as a forest, even in the center of town. Unlocking the iron courtyard gate, we saw that the neighborhood florist had left a pile of trash by her door: unsold bits of mistletoe, brown rotten wreaths, torn red ribbons, and empty plastic pots wrapped with crinkled silver foil. At the very bottom was a long fresh branch of spruce.

Margaret went closer to inspect the pile and gave a tug at the branch. It was larger than she

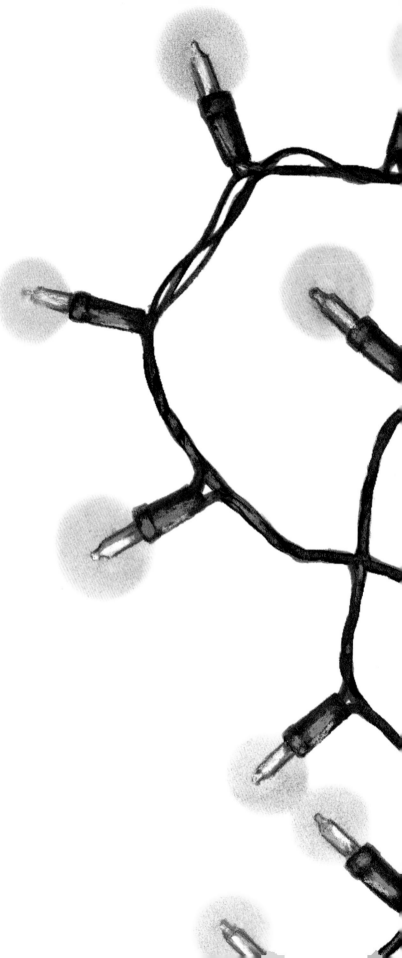

thought and so all three of us gave a good hard yank. Out came what was clearly the bottom of someone's too-tall Christmas tree, which they had chopped off and left for garbage. It was wide and bushy and shaped like a saucer. We pulled it completely free from the pile and hurried it inside the gate as if for fear that someone might reclaim it, then dragged it four flights up to the flat.

We were like triumphant gypsies, laughing and practically dancing the stump into the kitchen, the only room where it would fit. With a little imagination, it could almost be a tree, for it had the feel and scent and spirit of the day. We moved the table and chairs out into the hall, placed our tree in the largest pot we could find, then made the room a Christmas picnic ground, spreading a bright red quilt on the floor and placing candles on all the counters and window sills. But how to decorate? There were only the apples, hanging above.

"Pity we don't have popcorn and cranberries," said Margaret wistfully. "We always had yards and yards of homemade garlands on our tree when I was small."

"I always liked those paper chains," I said. "The kind you made in kindergarten, when you were six." Margaret and I looked at one another and smiled.

"I brought my sewing kit," she said, "and surely you have some drawers and boxes just full of interesting things. Perhaps we should have a look, and see what we can come up with."

The bottle of wine meant for Christmas was uncorked—for it was midnight by now—and we set to work. We pulled down a big box of odds and ends used for art projects and model making, got paper and glue and watercolors, took bits of saved ribbon, and whatever small, silly things we could find. I made a paper chain from old magazines, and Margaret strung a garland from buttons and hard candies. My boyfriend glued together bits of cardboard and string that, with a little paint, became flags and pigs and angels and hearts. We tied on ribbons and used paper clips as hangers and laughed aloud at the silly, wonderful things we had made.

"Oh, I had completely forgotten about these," Margaret said, digging to the bottom of her sewing kit and pulling out a small plastic bag. "I found them at a tag sale in Hyannis, and brought them to give to my friend Inga, the costume seamstress I met at the theatre. But I think we have a much better use for them here."

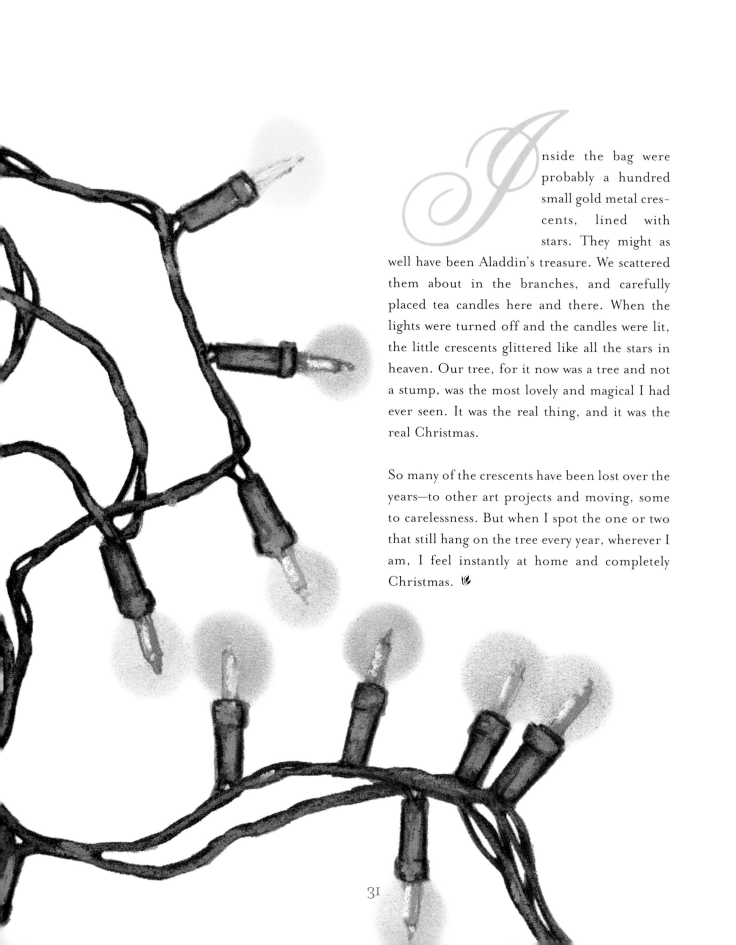

*I*nside the bag were probably a hundred small gold metal crescents, lined with stars. They might as well have been Aladdin's treasure. We scattered them about in the branches, and carefully placed tea candles here and there. When the lights were turned off and the candles were lit, the little crescents glittered like all the stars in heaven. Our tree, for it now was a tree and not a stump, was the most lovely and magical I had ever seen. It was the real thing, and it was the real Christmas.

So many of the crescents have been lost over the years—to other art projects and moving, some to carelessness. But when I spot the one or two that still hang on the tree every year, wherever I am, I feel instantly at home and completely Christmas. ❦

NICE KITTY

*I*t's not that he's really bad, or evil. It's just that, well…he attacks people. More that he scares them than really does anything…" my voice trailed off. "But some of our friends won't come in the house. And we do have a small child." The receptionist at the veterinarian's office was completely understanding. It was a slow day at the office, so she had plenty to say. It seemed there were many troubled cats in the city, and she knew them all. She speculated that holiday time might make things difficult, too, but I thought it was just a coincidence. She suggested it might be just a phase of rivalry with the toddler, or a food change, but I promised her it was not. This was not normal behavior for my cat. So she gave me the number.

"Cat therapist…Cat therapist? You're joking." I was a firm believer in the benefits of therapy— and I liked my veterinarian—but this was beyond the normal range of goods and services I expected a vet to recommend. I mean, I had considered the designer kitty coats, and bought the kitty toothpaste and the special food, but a therapist for cats? Well, it could help humans, so maybe…The cat had been so weird. And the holidays were coming, which meant we would have even more people in and out during the next two months. "How much?" I asked. The receptionist didn't know. That meant it was a sum even she didn't dare say aloud. "Let me call you back," I said.

That night, the cat trapped an unsuspecting guest in the bathroom. He stood outside the

door, back arched, fangs bared, yowling in that bloodcurdling cross between a baby and a demon from hell. Every time the door opened a crack, the cat would leap straight up, hissing for blood. We eventually threw a blanket over him, the guest escaped, and my mind was made up. I got the number from the vet and called.

"Hello...dear friends," said the tape. "Leave your name, your pet's name...and birthdate...and your phone and fax numbers, and I will get back to you as soon as possible." The pauses were punctuated with the sounds of chimes and the crash of ocean waves in the background, plus an odd squeal here and there. "Thank you...so much...for calling."

No message. There had to be a better way. Maybe some good old grocery-store cat food. Maybe he didn't really like that special order chow from the vet after all. And he hated having his teeth brushed.

The next morning, I stepped in a large puddle left by the cat in my closet. He had coughed up a truly disgusting hairball on my desk. He bit my leg when I walked past his bowl, and he scared the heck out of a delivery guy. My best friend refused to come over for dinner. Something had to be done. I called again, left a message, and waited a few days. Then he called: Frank Godard, Cat Therapist.

"So, let's talk a little bit about Rollo, shall we? You say he's aggressive, or passive-aggressive? Toward just you or anyone else?"

"Well, Fatty...."

"Excuse me? I am assuming here that you mean you call Rollo Fatty? This may be one of the contributing factors in his neurosis. Is Rollo overweight?"

"No, he's perfect. I mean in the weight department," I said, remembering that the vet had thought 21 pounds was a bit on the heavy side. "Well, he's pretty big, but it's just a nickname."

"Hmm," Frank said, "Clearly there are issues he has with his unstable identity in the house. Are you two alone, you and Fat...I mean Rollo? Uh-huh, you, your husband, and a small child. Yes, yes, classic sibling issues to work out. Clearly he feels threatened on many levels, unstable and likely to grow worse. You mentioned on the message that you've moved in the last six months. You must realize that this cat is living in a kind of hell!"

Oh, come on, I thought. How bad can it be? Mr. Godard thought it could be very, very bad.

"And," he added, "the holidays are approaching, which can only exacerbate things. Therapists always get more calls around this time of year. I think an immediate course of treatment is imperative. Luckily, I have an available session this Thursday afternoon. We can start working with the immediate family and then in later sessions bring in those especially targeted for attack."

"It may be just you, F...ollo and I this Thursday. Everyone else is out. Do we come to your office?" I asked, envisioning the dark red leather cat couch, a small box of shrimps for rewards, and wind-up mice for play therapy.

"Oh no, we need to have a clear picture of the home environment. So Thursday at 3:30, your place. I believe I have the address. The session's an hour and a half. Please block out the full time for both you and Rollo," he said. I heard the chimes in the background. "Goodbye. Don't worry, everything's...going to be just fine," he said soothingly.

Credentials? Somehow I had forgotten to ask. And I hadn't dared to ask the big question: How much? I managed to break the news to my husband that Rollo was going into counseling. "Is it voluntary or is this an intervention?" he laughed, and then saw my face. This was serious. "How much does this cost?"

"How much could it be for cats?" I said. "Besides, what can we do? Fatty is a public menace and it's important to get him calmed down by Christmas. There'll be so many people here." I paused. "Can we not tell anyone about this? I mean, just keep it in the family?"

"Ah. The mad kitty in the attic. No, believe me, I won't be mentioning it. Are you sure we really need to do this?" he asked. I nodded.

When Thursday rolled around, I was very nervous. A friend took the baby to the park. I cleaned the litter box and the cat dishes, and set out a can of Science Diet cat food to look respectable and caring. The doorbell rang. Fatty was napping, but I grabbed him and went to the door, petting furiously. "Welcome, Dr. ...umm, Mr. Godard. Please come in. This is Rollo."

*M*r. F. Godard entered, slowly reaching out his hand—to Rollo, I think, who immediately ran for cover. "Call me Frank." He was about forty, very pale, and I noticed he had claw marks all over his hands. He probably had treated cases much worse than Rollo—real hellions. Somehow that seemed a comfort. He carried a canvas satchel with him and, when we sat down, pulled out several books, notepads and two tape recorders. His pencil was a brand new Ticonderoga No. 2. Sharp. He asked me to get the cat and we would begin.

Rollo's back arched and he let out a low-pitched yowl, so he was bribed with catnip and a jingle mouse. Mr. Godard set up his tape recorders. There was the sound of chimes and waves crashing, just like his answering tape, and then those odd squeals. "Porpoise calls," he said, seeing my puzzled look. Chicken of the Sea, I thought. "I play and record simultaneously. You'll see. Testing 1-2-3...." There was a loud feedback squeal. Rollo tried hard to escape, but I held him fast.

"Nice kitty," said Mr. Godard into a microphone, nodding for me to continue petting the cat. "Nice kitty, Rollo. Nice kitty. Such a nice kitty." And all the while the strange nature symphony played in the background. "Nice kitty. What a pretty kitty. Such a good kitty."

This went on for forty-five minutes or more. I think both Fatty and I nodded out here and there. "Nice kitty. Nice, nice, nice nice kitty!" Mr. Godard said very emphatically, and snapped off the machines. I sat up.

"Was that it?" I was suddenly fully awake.

"Oh, no. This is just the beginning of our treatment. I want you to play this tape back as many times a day as possible for Rollo, at high volume in case he's sleeping. This is for the next month. Then call me and we can move on. I usually recommend six sessions to start, then an evaluation." He began packing things away, leaving a small pile of books and toys. "Now, these are some books you might want to purchase, written by myself, that will help you in this process. And I like to recommend these tapes of North Atlantic whale song and Amazon bird calls as a supplement to the tape we made. I think Rollo needs as intensive a treatment as you can give him. He seems very disturbed."

I looked down at the sleeping Fatty. "What's that little toy?" I asked, pointing to his pile of souvenirs.

"Oh, it's my very last catnip toy. From Asia. Called Catcat. Very powerful stuff. All the cats love them," he held it for a moment, then placed it before the sleeping Fatty. "My gift. Happy holidays."

"Do you think this will cure him?"

"I believe the treatment will help. Most certainly, I believe it will." He put on his coat and handed me a small square of paper. It was the bill. "This will cover the first two treatments of the six recommended sessions. Much cheaper than your therapy, I'm sure, haha! You may send a check if you wish," he said. "Goodbye, Rollo. Happy holidays." And he walked out the door. Such a trusting soul.

I did pay the bill. I played the tape a few times, then put it away. Rollo continued to attack two particular friends whenever they came over, and miscellaneous visitors if he was in a bad mood. At Christmas, we kept him in the closet. I changed vets. I threw away Frank Godard's phone number. And I took the little catnip toy and made an ornament. Not bad for $150. ❧

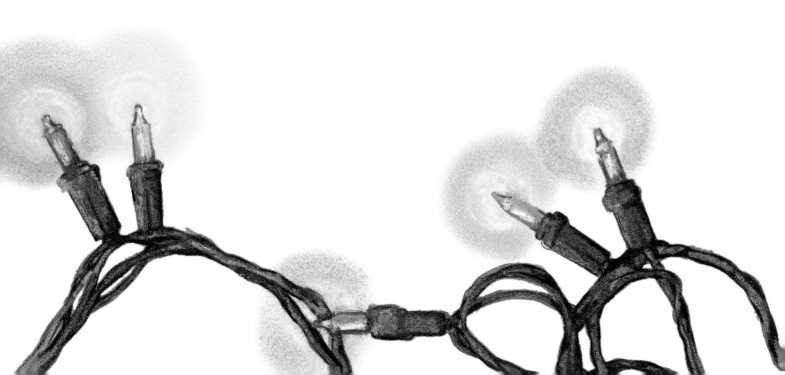

A STAR

That year was about platform shoes, tight pants, and dance clubs with mirrored balls suspended from their ceilings. It was heavy eye make-up and tight Lycra tops. Funkadelic. Everything shiny. It was about disco, and all of life had to have some glamour and should be very New York, even in the middle of Iowa. Naturally, the Christmas tree needed to reflect this wild and wonderful abandon. Please, nothing wooden or old or too sweet. It was clear that store-bought decorations wouldn't do—that season there seemed to be a plague of country craft ornaments my mother would have proclaimed "darling," and the fiber-wrapped red and green balls that were always unravelling, fuzzy and disgusting.

I would have to summon my creative resources and do it myself. In a few days there was to be a Christmas party at my place for some fellow students, a few professors, and assorted pals. It needed to be right—sparkling wine, French bread and cheese, and a disco explosion on the tree.

Sitting at the kitchen table late one night, all my art boxes and fabric scraps before me,

inspiration struck. Gold would be perfect: gold foil ornaments, gold mirrors, little stockings of gold lamé, tiny gold high heels, and tiny gold champagne glasses. It could be so beautiful! But I had nothing gold except some ribbon and a few scraps of matte gold paper.

Standing and stretching to some inspirational music—"Do You Want to Get Funky with Me"—

a flash of white at the bottom of the fabric box caught my eye. Pulling at the scrap, it turned out to be almost a yard of glorious shiny satin, left over from a tunic top made specifically to wear out dancing. My theme materialized: Stars, comets, moons, planets. The white satin interplanetary wonderland tree.

I set to work at once, feverishly making patterns and cutting as carefully as I could. The ornaments were ready to stitch together by 3:00 A.M. Unfortunately, due to some miscalculation and scissoring mishaps, there weren't quite as many as I had hoped. But with a dozen extra strands of twinkle lights, the tree could look spectacular. I flipped to the B side of Kool and The Gang and dragged the sewing machine from the depths of the front hall closet. Set up, plugged in, threaded, and oiled, it licked over the fabric in a flash. By 5:30, there was a galaxy of thirteen assorted stars and planets ready to stuff.

*A*ll the next day, the beautiful satin creations were visible in my mind's eye. I hurried into the fabric store right after class and bought polyester batting and gold cord to make the loops. The party was now just 24 hours away, and there was much to be done. I set to work stuffing each star and planet to the bursting

point, tucked in the golden cord, and hand-stitched them shut. In a few short hours, they were ready to hang, and it was then that I realized my choice of materials and lack of patterning skills had influenced the outcome more in the direction of *Captain Kangaroo's Playhouse* than Studio 54. The puffy fat stars and lumpy pillow planets had nothing slick about them. They had no sharp points, no edge, no glitter. They were so…soft. But it was too late to make alterations. The tree was completely nude. They would have to fly.

Next evening, as the party progressed, the stars somehow changed. With the music and light, the fizz of sparkling wine in plastic martini glasses, they began to look fabulous. And so did I, in three or four pounds of makeup, black three-inch platforms, my tightest, shiniest black pants, and to top it all off, my white satin disco tunic. It had long sleeves and a deep V-neck, with side slits to the waist. To me, it seemed elegant and yet somehow sexy. I floated among the guests, the disco Christmas queen.

I stood smiling before the satiny splendor of the tree, glass in hand, wobbling a bit from the combination of platforms and half a bottle of wine. One of the more distinguished guests, an associate professor from the east coast, came up to me with a big wondering smile on his face. I felt sure he must be dazzled by the incredible display on the tree—so creative, so contemporary, so *there*. I waited. He downed his glass, looked at me and then at the tree for a long silent moment, and then he winked. "I love it when the hostess has a dress that matches the ornaments," he said with the slightest, smallest breath of a New York accent. "It's so…Iowa!" 🌿

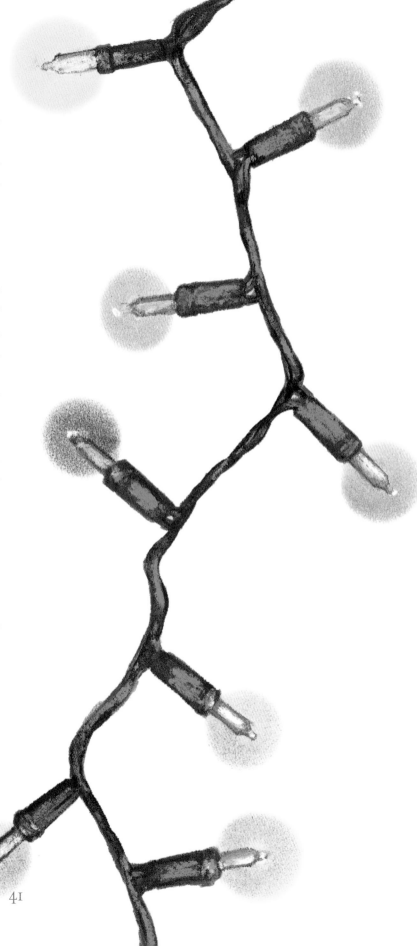

ACCESSORIES

There are more winter holidays every year. So says Celeste, long-time employee of a major department store and an old friend from grade school. This is nice if you have time for the festivities, but challenging if you work in retail. For one thing, you need to keep the sales promotions straight: the angel bear is for Christmas, but is the umbrella for Winter Solstice or was it ski goggles? Is the scented candle for Kwanzaa, and the mug for Hanukkah, or can you pick any of the above for $16.99 if you spend $150 by December 9, or was it spend $200 anytime and then the price drops to $7.00? It's all about numbers—and changing the decorations.

One year the store kept it simple. You received an exclusive faux jewel pendant if you spent so many dollars in accessories—jewels being appropriate for any holiday. And Celeste worked in accessories. She lived for accessories. She was perplexed at my inability to spend enough in her department to warrant a pendant or maybe two.

"You should have one for yourself and one as a gift for someone special," she said. "This is an exclusive piece, this pendant."

"It's not a pendant, it's a sculpture," I said. "Even my Aunt Shirley wouldn't wear it and she goes to Vegas three or four times a year. Who wears this stuff?"

"Everybody is wearing them. Don't you ever read *Vogue*? There was a Mardi Gras theme at the fall shows in Milan. People went crazy. And you simply must change your accessories to keep current. Besides, you can use it so many ways: as a pin, a pendant, on a big leather belt, a hair ornament. It's fabulous! It's the year's big statement."

"It's certainly big...and it's plastic."

"No, there's metal all around the edge, see? And plastic has been exonerated of its bad reputation. It's perfectly chic. Like microfiber."

"It's still plastic, and I still have to spend $75.00 to get something that's way, way too big and sparkly. Besides, Celeste, Mardi Gras is Lent."

"All the holidays just ooze together anyway. Wait a week, it's time to change your costume. Oh, come on...," her voice took on a pleading tone, "Help me out will you?"

I sensed an impending quota. "Are we talking numbers here?" I asked.

Celeste looked at her perfectly manicured hands, which were clutching each other for dear life, and leaned over the counter to whisper: "We were each given goals, and sales aren't what they should be. There are rumors of layoffs again. Serious layoffs. I really, really need the numbers or I am dead. The floor manager wants my face out of here, I know it." She nodded toward the next counter. "That's her, the thin, severe one in black. She hates me. She is pushing this pendant like there was a life attached to it. It's a terrible thing to do to the holidays, I don't care which one."

"I guess there are always a few more gifts I can buy, Celeste, but I can't do it today."

"Tomorrow?" she squeaked, staring at the floor manager. "Please?"

"That bloodthirsty, huh?" Celeste nodded nervously. "Okay, I'll try. Have you called everyone you know?" She nodded again. "Don't worry. You'll make it."

*C*eleste looked pale slumped against the pyramid of small handbags that rose in brilliant hues behind her. "This is my last December here. I can't take another holiday season in retail. It's become a war zone with twinkle lights. You spy on the other clerks. You sabotage their sales and then quickly scoop up the battered customers yourself. You rush to the men first because they spend more and buy faster. You wear low-cut necklines and too much make-up and this stupid smile day in and day out." She glanced down the counter to a man in a cashmere overcoat eyeing the bracelet case, and looked back at me with her Hollywood sales smile. Shoulders back, head held high. "Gotta go."

I gave her cold hand a squeeze and turned to walk toward the main entrance. I passed the floor manager, who for just a moment looked as terrified as Celeste, then composed her face into a mask of holiday cheer when she caught me looking. The door to the street was dripping with golden garlands, laden with jewels and ribbons and gilded fruit, a symbol of the season's abundance. It could almost, almost convince you of corporate benevolence and holiday good will. Once outside, the icy rain stung me back to reality. Celeste was in trouble.

When I returned to the store on Saturday afternoon, it was clear Celeste was desperate. She was constantly darting from one end of the counter to the other, trying to wait on everyone at once, keeping an eye peeled for new arrivals, checking every move with the floor manager, laughing too loudly. Handing over a check, I took the bag of overpriced gloves I had bought as gifts, and the red-and-gold box with the pendant.

"Maybe I can call some friends. I'm sure some of them will come in," I said hopefully.

"Oh, do," Celeste was near tears. "It's very close." She checked her lipstick in the mirror, practiced the full shark smile, then ran to nab the next customer before the other salesclerks had a chance. "Please help me!" she pleaded as she disappeared behind a six-foot Christmas tree of Isotoner gloves.

Later that day, I phoned everyone I could think to call. "You must stop in to see Celeste. Celeste is incredibly creative with gift ideas, and she can help anyone look fabulous for the holidays! You know it's all about accessories, and she is brilliant at suggesting just the perfect little accent for this season's look. And there's that exclusive pendant bonus straight from the Milan shows. Honestly, it makes a wonderful gift or a nice treat for yourself. And it's free...well, practically. I have one, and I love it! Celeste says they are flying out of the store, so you probably should stop in soon."

Everyone guessed the real story behind my big sales pitch. The news was splattered all over the papers every day, and it wasn't on the fashion page. Mergers. Layoffs. Chapter II. Numbers. So one by one, friends and family showed up at Celeste's counter and bought silver bracelets and gloves, silk scarves and little sequined evening bags to give to people who never went out. I found out Celeste had asked a few of them to make tiny complaints about the floor manager. And she somehow got every single customer to pendant level. By December 18, she was not only in the clear, her quota filled, but she had exciting news as well. She phoned that afternoon, breathless with excitement.

"Thank you so much for helping me. I made it. I did it. I love the holiday season! I love this store!"

"I thought this was your last December. You know, war zone, all that."

"Oh, I was just having a bad day when I said that. Because in the end, I won! They said I was the only one who made the numbers! I got a big bonus and now I'm the floor manager!"

"What happened to the other one?"

"Well, I should say co-floor manager. We'll be a team. The boss thought the department needed some new energy. An infusion. A fresh style. She needs me: she is last year's accessory."

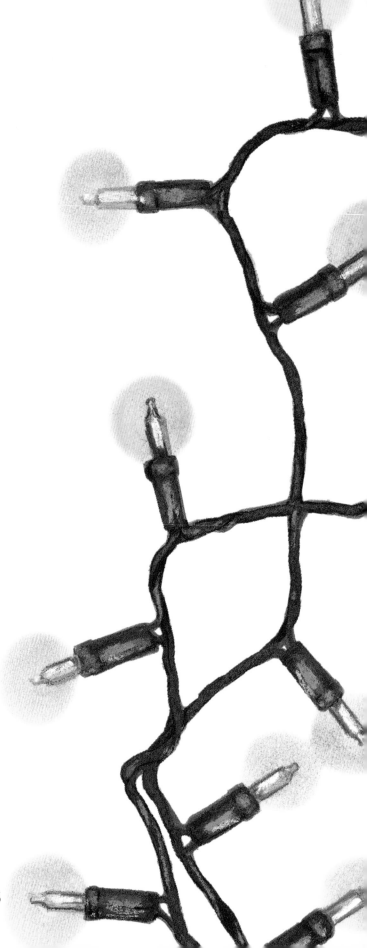

"Like the pendant."

"Oh, I'm so glad you like the pendant," Celeste went on at breakneck speed. "Isn't it brilliant? Doesn't it just say holiday? You know, this store is so much in the spirit that they gave everybody in the department an extra to take home as a holiday bonus. I'm wearing mine around the clock...because I honestly believe that besides being a fabulous accent piece, it's good luck. It's charmed. You should start wearing yours right away."

"I'm saving it for...for Lent. I think we should do penance for that poor floor manager." There was silence on the other end. "Really, Celeste, I heard what happened. It doesn't feel very Christmassy to me."

Celeste was defensive. "She didn't get canned, she's just getting the help she needs. And besides, she'll love working with me. I can really help her with the department." There was a short silence, and Celeste gave a little cough. "Okay, you're right. It wasn't nice, but I was scared and so was she. But it's Christmas now and we both came out of it all right. So why don't you lighten up? And wear that pendant. It saved my job and it cost you practically nothing."

"It all costs something, Celeste. Besides, it's too flashy."

"It's festive! Like an ornament."

"Bingo," I said flatly. "That's the only use for it."

"You're going to wear it to play Bingo?" Celeste paused. "We carry a hand-made silver charm bracelet that would be much more stylish, but I suppose a lucky pendant is perfectly okay. When is this Bingo thing, tonight?"

"No, Celeste," I said. "Tonight we're dressing the tree. And as you like to remind me, it's all about changing your accessories. I'll talk to you at Easter." ❧

THE ELF

The Elf was filthy when I found him in a flea-market shop a week before Christmas. I had stopped in a rush on my way home from work, looking for last-minute gifts. He was at the bottom of a cardboard box marked 25¢, full of cast-off toy parts and costume jewelry, hiding under some rhinestone and fake coral clip-ons. "He looks nasty," I said to the shopkeeper, a short, wiry woman of about sixty-two, with her dyed red hair pulled up in a messy French twist. She had a cigarette hanging from the corner of her mouth. "Good luck," she said, the cigarette nodding agreement with every word.

I assumed she meant the Elf. "Well, then he's got to be worth a quarter. I'll take him," I said.

"Wait a sec. He was in the wrong box," she said, jerking her head toward the front of the shop. She pulled at the chain holding her glasses around her neck, and set the spectacles on the end of her sharp little nose. "Lemme see." She walked to the front of the shop, her pink rubber flip-flops slapping time to the Christmas music on the radio. She led me to a table draped with a gold tinsel garland and some plastic holly, piled with holiday junk, and pointed to a sign that said CHRISTMAS TREASURES—$15.

"Fifteen bucks! That's a long way from a quarter!" I knew full well it was worth more than a quarter, but still..."What was it doing in the twenty-five cent box?"

49

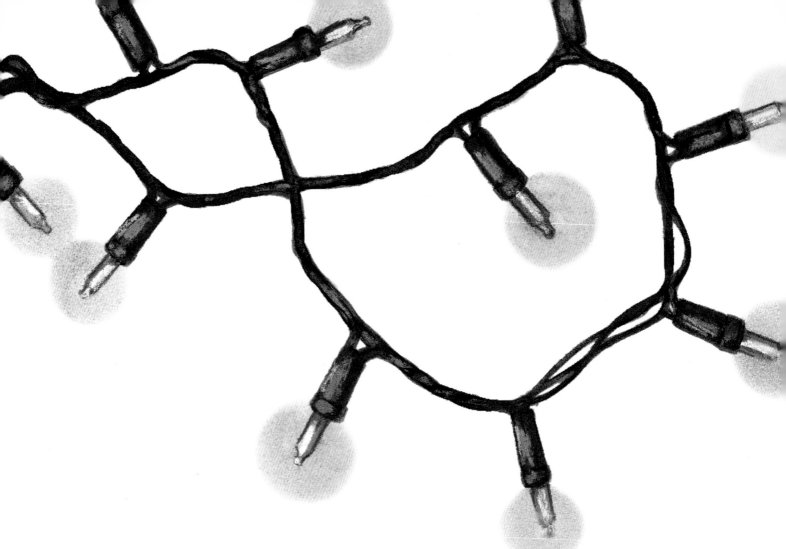

She just shrugged. "It's weird." She took the cigarette out of her mouth to light a fresh one, and said "Real collectible." She watched me from the corner of her eye, glanced carefully at my shoes, which happened to be stained, beat-up Aerosole loafers, and said, "Awright. Five."

"Sold." I said and handed her the cash. "I'm a little superstitious."

The lady wrapped the Elf in some tissue paper stained with coffee rings, and then placed him in an orange-and-white plastic sack that said SaveRite. She squinted at me over her glasses and gave me a queer smile. "Good luck," she said.

"And Happy Holidays to you," I returned cheerfully, already thinking about where to place the lucky Elf. My office needed lots of help in the luck department. In the baby's room? No, she might try to swallow it. By the bathroom scale! That would be a challenge for any good luck charm. It seemed best to start him off as a decoration on the tree. He was, after all, a Christmas Treasure—a Real Collectible. Probably worth lots more than five dollars. Definitely deserving of a prominent place: front of tree, placed at eye level. I couldn't wait to show him off.

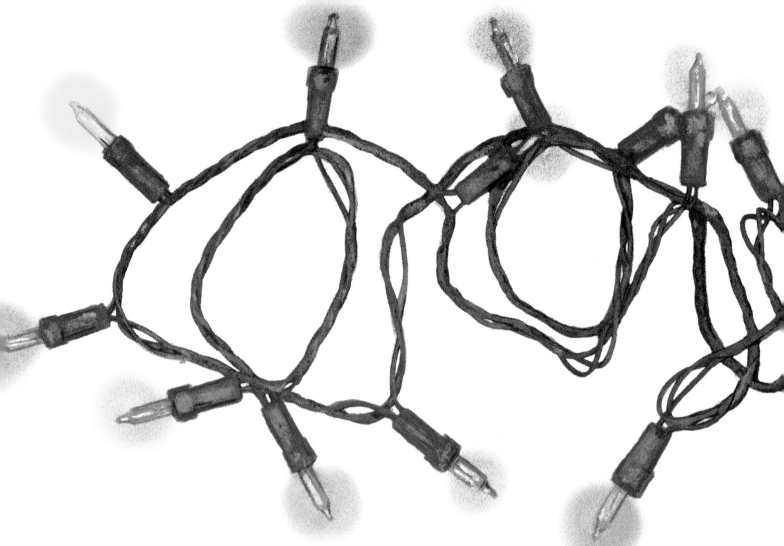

"He looks nasty," said the babysitter, taking a quick look on her way out the door. "I'd give him to someone you'd like to torment a little. Voodoo kind of thing. Like that horror movie toy...what's his name, uh...Chucky. Call him Chucky!"

"He's good luck!" I replied in protest. "The lady in the shop said so. And she gave me a great price, too. Five dollars."

"Oh Lord! You call that good luck? Get it out of here!" she rolled her eyes as she waved goodbye.

I passed it off as superstition, but there was something nice in her notion of making the Elf a gift. If I gave him to my husband, the good luck would stay in the family. I could wrap it up with a pretty ribbon and give it to him tonight over a nice dinner to start the Christmas week. The nice dinner would be a pleasant surprise in and of itself.

I gave the Elf a quick scrub with the dish brush and dried him on my skirt. Wrapped in a bright blue box with a curly red ribbon, he would make a cheery little present.

"No no, that's for Daddy," I said, as I grabbed the gift from the baby, who had managed to smash the box and put a few teeth marks in it for good measure. She started to wail at full volume as the phone rang. Daddy would be late. Forget the nice dinner: it would be dinosaur-shaped macaroni and cheese and some grapes. I put water on to boil and the package with the Elf up on a shelf. Now the cat was interested, too, and set out to claim the Elf for himself, tip-toeing across the stove and up among the canisters.

*B*aby was still demanding the package at full volume when Daddy came up the stairs. The cat had succeeded in reaching the package while I was changing a diaper, and managed to dump the sugar in the process. He had bitten off four or five inches of curling ribbon, which at that moment came back up onto the rug, mixed with the Friskies Salmon he had for dinner. The phone rang again: magazine sales. No thank you. The smell of scorched cheese began to fill the house.

"Merry Christmas week," I said, handing my husband the gift as he walked through the door. He looked at the gnawed-off ribbon and the bashed-in box. "It's good luck," I promised.

He opened it at once. "He looks nasty."

"It's good luck," I insisted. "I thought we'd celebrate the beginning of Christmas week, and he can be the first one on the tree. Hang it quickly, though, will you, so the cat doesn't bite off the cord and throw up again. Want some macaroni and cheese, or should I order in?" He shook his head no, then yes, and gave the Elf to the baby, who put it immediately into her mouth. Within thirty seconds, her lips were bright red.

"For God's sake, get that thing, will you!" I yelled. "It's probably lead paint!" That prompted a huge tantrum. The burner left on under the macaroni set off the smoke alarm. The phone rang again; a business call this time. Daddy handed me the baby and disappeared into the other room.

"Good luck. Right." I looked at the Elf, and hung him high up on the back of the tree, out of sight. Magically, within the hour, the cat had stopped gagging, the baby was asleep, the phone stopped ringing, and the carry-out Chinese food had arrived. Silent night.

"See?" I said to my husband, pointing toward the tree. "He works like a charm."

We spent the next couple of hours adding decorations to the tree and even feeling a little festive, then went off to bed. At 2:00 in the morning, the tree fell over. The floor was littered with pine needles, hooks and broken bits of plastic and glass. "It's got to be him," said my husband. We looked for the Elf as we resurrected the tree, but he was nowhere to be found. I was secretly relieved, then forgot about him completely.

The whole holiday week was lovely—almost too good to be true. Beautiful weather. Thoughtful gifts. Delicious food. Lots of friends and family. In January, when I dragged the tree to the curb for the trash collectors, I spied a flash of red deep in the branches. There is always an ornament that goes missing. I reached in and pulled it out: It was him. I grabbed for the garbage can lid. Such a nice Christmas, I thought, the lid poised in mid-air. I stuffed the Elf into my jacket pocket and brought him back inside. 🌿

BIG BALLERINA

"Big. Really big," I heard someone mock whisper. It was Christmas Day, and friends had gathered for a festive dinner. Feasting is a big part of the holidays, and while any celebration will have its tango of temptations and elastic waistbands, Christmas is open season on anything edible, especially anything containing F-A-T. Somewhere, deep down, we are all conscious of the ultimate effect of all this indulgence. We all feel a teeny-weeny, tiny bit guilty about the fourth helping of sausage-stuffed mushrooms, the giant gingerbread boy, the cheese dips, but no one wants to hear the admonishments spoken aloud.

We were munching hors d'oeuvres, waiting for the potatoes to boil, the gravy to be made. Everyone was hungry. "Bigger than last Christmas, there's no doubt about that," someone else said to the accompaniment of loud laughter. Who were they talking about? I hurried back into the kitchen to attend to the gravy.

My backside bumped into the counter on my way to the stove. It was a small kitchen, but cozy, and everything smelled lovely: a huge butter-basted turkey, two kinds of potatoes, sausage and cornbread stuffing, fresh cranberry relish, three kinds of homemade bread, creamery butter, four vegetables, soup, cheeses, fruit, fourteen desserts counting all the kinds of cookies, boxes of chocolates and candies, real cream for the coffee, three kinds of wine, liqueurs. It was everything you could possibly want and I wanted it all.

But what was that I had heard about big? I checked all the pots and pans, then returned to where the guests had gathered to admire the ornaments on the tree. I tried for a stealthy approach in order to eavesdrop.

"Those legs are hilarious with that short little skirt." Okay, maybe it was a little short, I thought as I tugged down my skirt, but let her without bulge throw the first scone. I heard the sound of potatoes boiling over in the kitchen and turned too quickly, knocking into the tree and sounding an alarm of tinkling bells. "Look at that bottom!" The comment trailed me like a heat-seeking missile into the next room.

I twisted the burner knob under the potatoes to low. Christmas was supposed to be a time of unbridled feasting and merriment, not figure analysis, I thought in disgust. I had seen the damned holiday fat chart they print in the paper every year. I knew that eggnog was a sin against humanity. I knew ChexMix belonged in the Dark Ages. I knew bacon-wrapped chicken livers could cause a swimsuit, carefully packed away in the closet, to self-combust. And here I was making gravy without pouring off all the fat. But for heaven's sake! Maybe I could make a quick salad....

The bubbling pan of gravy sent clouds of fragrant steam up to my nose and made my arm whisk on automatic pilot until it was a smooth, brown, delicious lake waiting to run down the white mountains of mashed potato. There was the sound of raucous laughter in the other room. I jerked the heat to a simmer and slammed the lid onto the pan.

"Dinner in ten minutes! Can I get some help, please?" I bellowed. This brought a rush of assistants to the kitchen and a hubbub of activity around the table. Oohs and aahhs were heard, groans of anticipation, small curses at having chosen tailored garments. And still a giggle or two here and there about "Big."

*P*ortion control is everything, I thought, placing a molehill of mashed potatoes, a dribble of gravy on my plate. I added only a few tablespoons of cranberry sauce. "No stuffing, thanks." I passed the heavy, redolent bowl quickly to the left. I took just three ounces of turkey, white meat only. No homemade rolls. Definitely no butter. Had no one thought of a relish tray? All the vegetables were 1950s classics: cheesey, creamy, and strewn with crunchy fried onions. I sighed.

"Feeling okay?" someone asked.

I nodded. "Hungry."

"Well I would hope so—it's Christmas dinner. Laugh and be fat! Think of Santa Claus! Frosty! Burl Ives!"

The bowls revolved around the table a second time, as the crowd responded to the holiday challenge. I abstained, thinking instead of Tiny Tim, the Little Match Girl, and Rudolph, who was probably kept on short rations for being an oddball. The bowls went around a third and a fourth time, in a dizzying waltz of plenty.

"Shouldn't you be eating more?" someone asked. I shook my head no, and drank six or seven glasses of water. "Gosh I'm full! Let's go out and sit by the tree," I said, rising slowly and waddling into the next room. I heard giggling from behind me, along with mock groans as someone said "I feel so...big!"

I turned to face the guilty parties: "I know I'm big! I know it! But it's Christmas. I want to enjoy my holiday. I couldn't even eat dinner. All I've heard all evening is big, big legs, big bottom. Please...."

The girls looked completely stunned. "You *are* big. Even you have to admit that. But did you think we were talking about you?"

"Well, I am feeling awfully sensitive about this extra forty-five pounds...."

"But you're seven months pregnant for God's sake! You look fabulous. And so does she," They pointed toward the tree. "The big ballerina."

I approached the tree, and on the end of a branch hung a ballerina, twirling slowly on a long silken cord. She was new that year, sent by a friend traveling through Spain, and I hadn't really taken a good look. She was brilliantly colored, shiny, happy, and quite fat. She seemed a little silly at first, not at all your standard issue ballerina. But dance she would, joy in every step. The big ballerina was a symbol of the season, and a reminder to me: Holidays are for joy, music, dancing, and seconds. They pass quickly by—the moments and the meals. Don't let them get away without enjoying them to the fullest!

"Oh, I see," I turned to the girls, smiled, and paused a beat. "Do you all want dessert right away, or can I finish my dinner? 🌿

She lifted the lid from the box slowly. It was one of those white cardboard gift boxes from a long-defunct department store in Chicago. Inside were wads of tissue and Styrofoam pellets. Her rough, bony hands shook slightly as she peeled away the layers, until finally she hooked her middle finger through a black thread loop and held up a glittering, silver-colored glass bird. It was shiny, but not the shine of cheap plastic or chrome. It had a deeper shine, somehow reflecting time as well as light. It twirled lazily in the air, its wings and tail a shimmer of glass threads. "You see, it does fly!" she crowed triumphantly. "You must hang it on the tree where there is plenty of room to move. It's a creature that demands its freedom, even tethered to a string."

She lifted her pale, thin arm high in the air, as fragile as a dry branch that might crack at the slightest breeze. The silver bird swung now in a wide arc, still turning as it flew. She grabbed it with her other hand.

"It had been hidden for years. But it was always mine. I remember when this bird first came to me, one Christmas so long ago. I must have been nine or ten. Even then the bird was old, or old to me. I think of these things differently now, of course." She moved slowly to the sofa and sat down, as if a quick movement might startle the bird.

"It was born in Austria, my bird. I say born because it was born out of the breath of some glass blower, an artist who gave it form and iridescent feathers, these wings that somehow translate flight into matter. The bird was sent to a shop in Vienna to be sold for the holiday season. The shop was called Gutterman's. I remember their name from the beautiful box: gray felt, with red printing so thick you could feel it with your fingertips. There was a coat of arms stamped at the top in gold, of two bears and a lily. I have no idea if it meant the Guttermans were royalty, or purveyors to royalty, or if it was just a gimmick. But it looked altogether splendid to me. Inside it was lined with watered silk, also red, and had a satin band to hold the bird still. The box alone would have proved sufficient as a gift, but when I opened it and saw the bird, I was completely dumbfounded. Father knew I loved birds. I was always out scattering crumbs from the breakfast table, and Mother would scold me for bringing round the pigeons."

he gave the bird a twirl. "It's true the pigeons were messy, but once in a while you'd get meadowlarks, or a bluebird, even mourning doves. I didn't know all their names, but I liked to see them swoop down onto the walkway and peck at our biscuits, still buttery and soft. I would have liked those crumbs myself a few years later, after Father was gone and times were hard. There was the war, and everything changed in a flash. But you can't go picking at the past." She placed the bird on her lap and stroked its tail.

"But why do you say it was hidden?"

"It was hidden by my mother for many years. Father had given it to me, but my younger sister, your Great-Aunt Gen, claimed that it was hers. Our constant bickering every year made Mother decide to put it away. She said once that she had sold it, but I wept so bitterly she admitted that in fact she was saving it for when I married and had a house of my own. It was my link to a beloved past that had otherwise disappeared. When I told Genevieve this, she was furious. Mother tried to explain that there were other things from the old house that were meant for her, but Gen insisted the bird was hers. Well, of course, we grew up and moved away, and forgot all about it. When Mother died, Gen went first to the house to clear up. I was busy with my own family by that time, and so I never knew what was in the attic or the closets. It wasn't until perhaps six or seven years later, when we were spending Christmas with Gen and her family, that I spied the bird hanging on her tree. She knew I knew, but didn't say

a word. And neither did I. We had been brought up to be...discreet. And very, very stubborn. The following year, Gen had a trimming party and I asked specifically to hang it. Gen seemed a little flustered, but found the bird, which was now stored in a plain brown box, and showed me where it should be hung. I asked about the beautiful gray box with the red-and-gold trim. She claimed it had disappeared; didn't I remember that Mother had thrown it out, that it was all covered with mildew? No, I didn't remember that, I told her politely. I did dig around in the ornament boxes that year, hoping I would see it, but it was not to be found. At least I had the bird. I mean, I knew the bird could still be caught."

"What do you mean by that?" I asked, sipping a glass of Grandma's best kirsch.

"I mean it was mine and I meant to have it. If she wouldn't give it to me, then I would find a way to make the bird fly away on its own. And I did." She held it in her opened palm, like a pet, and spoke to it. "Isn't that right?"

"Now you're getting loopy, Gram. How does a glass bird fly?"

"It's a matter of setting the stage. And preparing the audience. One Christmas your grandfather and I spent with Gen and Fredrick, we brought two lovely bottles of port, which they drank to the bottom. I pretended to have a few glasses, too. The lights were low, only the tree and some candles, a fire in the fireplace. I went up to the tree to spin the bird, as I did every year, only this time as I spun it, I acted as though I was wildly intoxicated, and swung the bird too high. As it lifted in the air, I caught the string with my one hand and threw a silver ball to the floor with my other. Crash! In the confusion, the bird flew right into my pocket and, frightened to death, refused to emerge. I apologized profusely. Genevieve was too tipsy to notice there were no tail feathers in the debris—she's never read a mystery in her life— and went immediately to bed in a state. We weren't invited to Christmas the next year. Or the year after that. Your Grandfather was confused why Gen and I were no longer on speaking terms: he knew about the bird, but couldn't possibly understand what it meant. I hadn't let him in on my scheme, so consequently, the bird was forced into hiding again. Eventually my clumsiness was forgiven, or rather, it was tolerated in the interest of the nieces and nephews. One year, Gen hosted a big family Christmas party. I passed by her little sewing room on my way to the bathroom, and what do you think I just happened to see? Way up high on the topmost shelf, filled with buttons. Gray felt, with red and gold printing."

"Oh, you didn't, did you?" I grimaced.

"But it didn't exist, remember? Mother had thrown it out, so who was to say?" She hung the bird on a long branch that swept out over the rest, and pushed the ornament into its arc of flight. "It's silly, really, how the smallest things can create a space as big as the sky if you let them. And then you're not sure how you'll ever get home." She watched the bird swing gracefully through the air, then turned to me. "Meanwhile, my bird needs a new perch. I'm not going to be around much longer, and a bird shouldn't be kept in a box, no matter how pretty. I think your tree will do nicely."

"Oh, Gram, how lovely. Knowing it was yours when you were small, and the shop in Vienna— I'm thrilled to have it. Thank you so much...but," I said. "Maybe you should tell Aunt Gen."

"Tell her what? That your grandmother gave you a bird just like hers? That we are both ridiculous old ladies, acting like fools? No, no. If I tell her anything, it might be that birds cannot be held. Time flies. Life flies. A flutter and crash." She finished her glass of brandy and yawned. "It's awfully late, isn't it? Perhaps next Christmas I'll give her back the buttons." 🌿

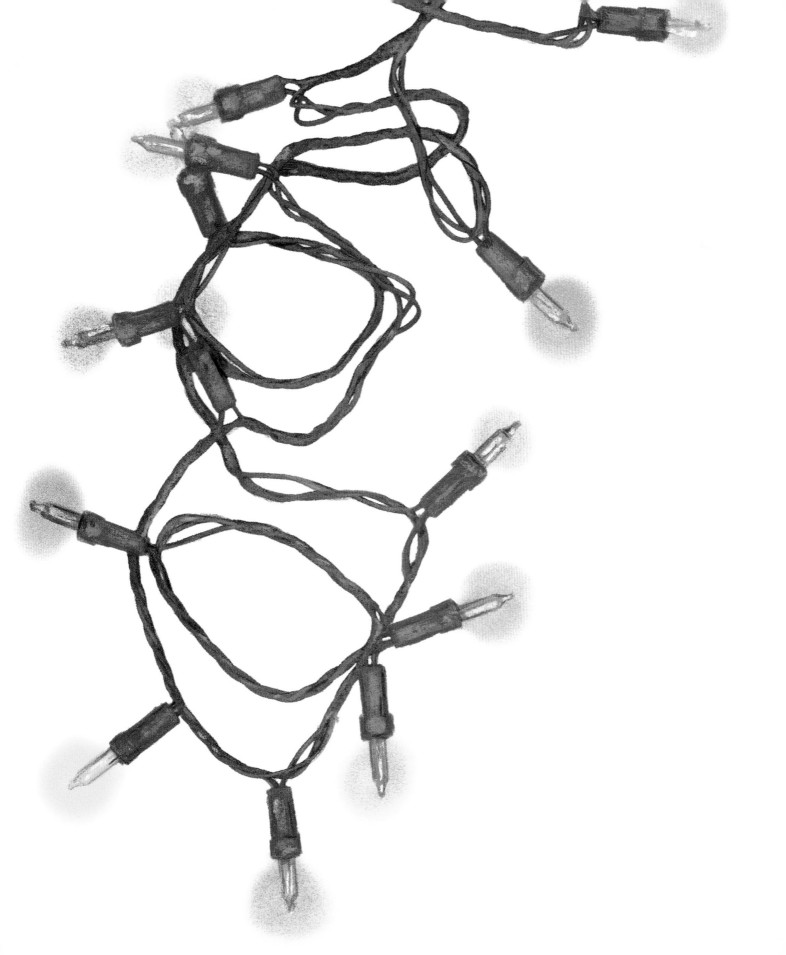

WINGS

*F*ame and ornament are a perfect pair of words. Especially when I think of the ornament making contest. It began small, as something fun for our guests to do while waiting for the turkey to roast. To everyone's surprise, the results were amazing: each ornament a creative delight. The contest was so popular, we decided to make it an annual event. There is a winner every year, and like the Academy Awards, it is a vote of one's peers. So intense is the competition that people have been known to vote for themselves in the not-so-secret written balloting. And there is always a prize, like Batman bubble bath, or the fabulous Astro Bank, batteries included. But the real battle is for honor and glory. To win is to achieve a shimmering place in Yuletide history, at least at our house.

In the fourth year of the competition, the theme seemed to bring out a special fervor in our friends. The subject was movies. It could be any movie, the end result just had to hang on the tree. The participants had squeezed into a tight circle on the bedroom floor, transformed into the arts-and-crafts room for the occasion. In the center of the circle were piles of paper, bits of junk and tinsel, model parts, balsa wood, paints, glitter, knick-knacks, beads, and what-nots to transform into something new and, if not beautiful, then at least thought-provoking to put on the tree. The guests, adults all, were digging hysterically in the piles, grabbing and pulling, and hoarding while trying to innocently lift things from their neighbor's stash. Forget good will toward men.

After this initial chaos, the room became the center of silent, serious business. There was only an impatient sigh heard now and again from someone waiting for the glue gun or a paint brush. Then the intense quiet of creativity was broken by the insistent razz of the downstairs buzzer. I went to open the door.

It was Eric, breathless and red-faced from his trek from another party up the street. He wore a leather varsity jacket in primary colors, a brilliant multi-colored scarf with matching mittens he had knitted for himself, and a forest-green stocking hat with attached antler horns, complete with red flashing lights. His glasses were completely fogged over and he carried a beautiful little basket of jelly donuts and gold-wrapped chocolate coins. He was a holiday ornament all on his own.

"Happy Hannukah," he said. "I know it's a multi-cultural crowd here."

"Semi-cultural, maybe. We're finishing up on the ornament contest and the theme is movies. If you hurry, you can get an entry done before we sit down to dinner."

"Oh, I just wanted to stop by for a minute. I have another party to get to for dinner, but I would love to enter the contest," he said, handing me his things and changing to a smaller but equally colorful stocking hat. "Your place is freezing!" he added, but I knew he felt awkward, his hair almost completely gone.

Eric greeted the rest of the crowd and set to work. He seemed to know exactly what he wanted and found all the pieces right away. Most of the others had finished, but there were always one or two obsessive perfectionists who would paint halfway through dinner. By the time we had heard the Karen Carpenter holiday tape twice, the event was declared closed. Since Eric had to leave, we held the judging without delay.

Part of the contest was guessing the title. The first few entries were mildly amusing, but either too obvious or incomprehensible: *Please Don't Eat the Daisies*, *Nosferatu*, *Vertigo*, *Gone With the Wind*, *Grease*. *Carrie*, and *Last Year at Marienbad* made more challenging entries. There was an elaborate tribute to *Funny Girl* complete with the leopard coat, and an impressive *Silence of the Lambs* that was officially disqualified for its size (too big to hang) and unofficially disqualified for content, and a stunning *Sunset Boulevard*, complete with a turbanned Gloria Swanson chauffeured by Erich Von Stroheim in the Dusenberg. Then there was Eric's.

He held it up and shook it. It jingled softly. We all looked at him with blank faces. He shook it again and waved it in the air, all feathers and bells. "Don't you get it?" he asked.

We started to guess: *The Bells of St. Mary's, Bells Are Ringing, Bell Book and Candle, Belle de Jour, For Whom the Bell Tolls, The Birds, Birdie, Bye Bye Birdie, Bird Man of Alcatraz, Wings, Angels in the Outfield, The Trouble with Angels, Heaven Can Wait.* "You're getting warmer!" he said.

The crowd was stumped. "It's Christmas. Bells. Wings...it's impossible that you don't get this," he said. He held it up and jingled the ornament one last time. "Everytime you hear a bell ring, it means some angel has just got his wings."

We groaned in unison: *"It's a Wonderful Life...."*

"Yes, it is," he replied. "And I would love to stay for dinner, but I am just stopping here between parties and I have to go." He handed me his ornament and got his things from the closet. "Just leave a message on my machine so I know where to claim the prize. Merry Christmas to all. God bless us every one." He placed his antler hat back on his head and went out into the night.

Sunset Boulevard was the winner that year by one vote, even though it, too, was slightly oversized. But I hung the Wonderful Life wings in a better spot. And when we took down the tree, it went into the box with the winning ornaments from previous years, to be proudly displayed the following season. Eric died three months later, a victim of AIDS. His ornament is hung on our tree every Christmas, and even though one of the wings has disappeared and the bow is slightly wrinkled, the bells jingle sweeter each year. 🍃

here should be at least one on every tree, or maybe a dozen or two. I am thinking of cookies: All the wonderful Christmas cookies made at home or at school, or day care, or church. Some cookies are so tempting that they never make it past the kitchen. But many deserve a place on the tree—either for their beautiful decorations and festive shapes, or for the thought behind the making of them. One I always hang on the tree is burned and lumpy, dotted with red hots and knotted with a loop of frayed ribbon. It doesn't fall in the pretty category, and you can't eat it, but it is oh so sweet. It was cut from some special pre-school dough by my then three-year-old child, and it makes me think of the cookie cycle. If you've ever done any Christmas baking at all, you know what this means.

Around the first of December, in millions of homes, it begins. There are recipes clipped from magazines, calls made to mothers and aunts and friends who can bake. There are special expeditions to the store. The cart fills up with huge bags of flour and sugar, vats of Crisco, vanilla, cinnamon, cardamom, ginger, butter, butter—and butter. The bottle of molasses you think will last a decade, the candied fruits, red hots, silver dragees, almond extract, chestnut paste. There are debates over walnuts versus pecans, cocoa versus baker's chocolate, discussions on the merits of non-stick, tips in the hunt for the perfect gingerbread boy form, and have you bought a gingerbread girl yet?

All this happens slowly, like the season's turn. Then suddenly there you are at the pinnacle of the process: the two days set apart for the job. Day one is mixing day. Straightforward, if you have done the shopping and your recipe homework. The children are busy or sleeping. The electric mixer hums in the night-lit kitchen for what seems like hours. The sharp crack of eggs. Measuring is critical, and carefully scrutinized. It's high science. At least once or twice you are sure that you forgot the baking powder. Or the vanilla. And if the recipe is tripled or quadrupled, as it really should be, did you put in half the sugar or twice as much? And what exactly does cream of tartar do, anyway? This effort results in a huge bowl of sticky yellow dough left to chill overnight, a formless mass waiting to be rolled and pounded and cut into a new identity.

Everyone in the house knows when cookie day has come. Sometimes the neighbors, too, for there might be playmates invited to join in. The time has been set for evening, when everyone is home. Once dinner is done, the dough comes out, along with the pans, the rolling pin, the pastry cloth, waxed paper, spatulas and knives, the shiny cutters in their special box, and jars and jars of sprinkles and candy decorations.

The mixer hum is heard again as icing is prepared, thick and snowy white, waiting to be dyed into a rainbow of colors.

The biggest child gets to roll the dough. Cold still, it needs just a sprinkle of flour to lie flat, and soon the wide circle is ready to cut. The smallest child cuts the first cookie, usually somewhere in the very center, a ritual gesture of plenty. It gets practical later.

When the circle of dough is cut full of shapes, the outside corners are lifted slowly, a lacy border pulled up to reveal the first batch: reindeer, snowmen, bunnies, stars, elves, and Christmas trees. Somehow each cookie is slightly different, in spite of their common mold. A child can easily see the ones he or she has cut: slightly bigger antlers, drooping hat, missing paw, crooked star, thumbprint.

When that first pan enters the oven, there is an undercurrent of nerves. Did all the flour go in? Were they rolled too thick? Too thin? Is the temperature right? Ding! The timer sounds, and through the oven door window the cookies look...perfect! A rush of heat and aroma escapes when the pan is lifted out to cool. The next sheet of cookies can enter. And that part of the process is put full speed ahead, with rolling and patting and cutting. Heavy balls of thick, sticky dough transformed into thin, delicate shapes, crisp and delicious.

Decorating soon begins. Fingers turn pink and green and red with frosting, snitching a taste of all the little candies. Someone asks every time: Why *can't* we eat the little silver balls? Only the adults use raisins and almonds. There are rainbow sprinkles everywhere. The broken cookies are quickly eaten. The counter starts to fill with magical treats. The little ones drift off. The older children work on for a while, then, overcome by night and too much sugar, they head for bed. Soon it is just Mother, using the last ball of dough scraps to finish the job, clean the bowls and pans, turn the oven off, sweep up the mess. In the stillness, the kitchen is overfull with color and scent.

The cookies are magic for a time, and taste delicious through all of December. You can, at least for a few days, recognize the ones you've made. After New Year's, though, they lose their taste. Out they go, no more to be seen until the cycle begins again.

But even the cookie cycle exists inside of a larger circle. As the next year rolls around and the next, the older kids have jobs and homework. The younger ones take over, then they grow up, and suddenly, one year, no one is home. It becomes a chore. The cookie cutters get put away and can't be found. No one has the time or inclination. Everyone is dieting. The cookie cycle ends...for a time. Because soon there are new children who need to know. Who need to smell those smells. And see what it's like to eat raw dough and not get worms, lick beaters and bowls and fingers and feel almost sick...but not too sick to eat hundreds and hundreds and hundreds of cookies. To see that lump of plain dough shaped with their own small hands into something beautiful and delicious. To make something so wonderful you'll hang it on the tree. To remind you that the cookie cycle never ends. 🌿

❦ THANK YOU ❦

Many thanks to the people who helped to realize this book: Marta Hallett and Elizabeth Sullivan for giving it a home; Tricia Levi for shepherding it along with patience and good humor; Stephany Evans for her advice and assistance, and Marisa Bulzone for her sensitive editing. On a more personal level, thanks and love to the many people who have played a big part in making Christmas something worth writing about for me: Mom and Dad; Margaret; Grandma Foley and the entire wacky Foley clan; all the Engelmanns, especially Ailleen, Rick, Gary, Matt, Jeff, Huck, and Brian; Grandma Abbie; assorted in-laws of the best kind; cousins, neices, and nephews; Michele and Cotra; Martha, Ricky, Jeffrey, Jim, Sharon, DeeDee, Eric K; in Sweden: Inga Britt och Willy Walldov, Lassie and Lars, Ursula, Agneta, Christer, Dan, Christoph, Ulf and the Pepparkaksmor; all the assorted visitors, friends and neighbors who have passed through during the holidays; my naughty elves Lilly and Nia; and most of all to Erik, my own private Santa.

❦ ABOUT THE AUTHOR ❦

Karen Engelmann was born and raised in Iowa, then moved to Sweden where she worked as an illustrator and designer for eight years. Upon returning to the United States and rediscovering English, writing became a secret passion—which became public when her first book, Great Expectations—A Meditative Journal for Mothers-to-Be, *was published in 1997.* Visions of Angels, *a photography book which she created with Nelson Bloncourt, was published in the fall of 1998.* Ornaments *is her first book of short stories.*